By Mary Man-Kong
Based on the original screenplay by Elise Allen

Special thanks to Rob Hudnut, Tiffany J. Shuttleworth, Vicki Jaeger, Monica Okazaki, Luke Carroll, Anita Lee, Julie Puckrin, Walter Martishius, Derek Goodfellow, Pam Prostarr, Aeron Kline, Conrad Chow, Lester Chung, Allan Pantoja, Kelsey Ayukawa, Eric Wong, Greg Montgomery, Ryan Singh, Sarah Miyashita, Winston Fan, Karl Bildstein, and Sean Newton

A Random House PICTUREBACK® Book
Random House 🏠 New York

Far away in a magical place called Flutterfield was a kingdom of butterfly fairies. The fairies didn't like when the sun went down because they were afraid of the hungry Skeezites who came out at night. Luckily, Queen Marabella had filled the trees with magical glowing flowers to protect the butterfly fairies. As long as Marabella lived, there would be light in Flutterfield.

One pretty fairy named Mariposa was different from all the other fairies. She liked the dark sky because she loved to study the stars. "Look," Mariposa said as she pointed out a constellation to her best friend, Willa. "There's the Archer's bow and arrow."

Mariposa and Willa worked for two bossy siste
named Rayna and Rayla.

"Mariposa, you have to beflutter all my gowns
before the palace ball tonight," cried Rayna.

"And I need sparkly thistleburst for my hair,"
demanded Rayla. "The prince needs to see me sh
After helping the two sisters get ready, Maripos
and Willa flew off with them to the ball.

Willa was eager to go to the ball. But Mariposa didn't want to go inside because she didn't think she'd fit in. The queen's royal assistant, Henna, tried to convince her, but Mariposa felt more comfortable studying the stars and reading her book.

Mariposa thought Henna was a very kind fairy—but she wasn't! Henna was secretly plotting to take over Flutterfield and had poisoned the queen with an evil potion.

Mariposa flew around looking for a place to read—and bumped into Prince Carlos! The prince was impressed by Mariposa's knowledge of the stars and her interest in faraway places.

After the ball, Prince Carlos asked Mariposa for help. "The queen is very sick," said the prince. "Soon Flutterfield's lights will go out and we will all be in danger. Can you take this map and find the cure?"

Mariposa agreed, but she couldn't do it alone.

When Rayna and Rayla heard about Mariposa's special mission, they volunteered to help so they could impress the prince.

Soon Mariposa and the sisters had flown far beyond Flutterfield's protective lights—and Skeezites were everywhere! To make matters worse, Rayna had lost the map!

Remembering that they needed to go east to the Bewilderness, Mariposa followed the stars to find it. There they met a cute and playful creature named Zinzie. Zinzie led the fairies to two mermaids who knew where the cure was.

But the mermaids were selfish and only agreed to help if they could get rare Conkle Shells in return. Mariposa and the sisters dove into the water and quickly found the shells—but woke the Sea Beast! Luckily, the fairies worked together and swam in different directions to outsmart the monster.

"Fly with the arc of the sun and you will find the cure in the Cave of Reflection," the mermaids said as they swam off with the Conkle Shells.

After flying for hours, the fairies reached the Cave of Reflection. The tiny Fairy Speck told them that the cure was hidden behind a star in the sky.

"The Archer is a navigator in the sky," said Mariposa. "His arrow points to the correct star."

"Are you sure?" asked the Fairy Speck. "That star is all alone and is meaningless."

"Every star is there for a reason," said Mariposa. "They don't have to fit in to be important. They just have to be themselves."

When Mariposa chose the lone star, it transformed into the cure—and Mariposa's wings magically grew larger and more beautiful.

With the cure in hand, the friends rushed to save the queen!

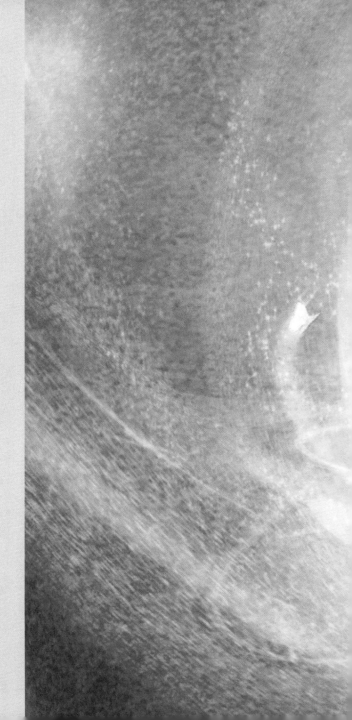

Back at the palace, Henna took control of the kingdom with her horrible Skeezites. Prince Carlos tried to stop them, but there were too many.

Suddenly, Mariposa and her friends arrived.

"You've never felt like you belonged in Marabella's kingdom," Henna told Mariposa, trying to trick her. "But you will in mine. Everyone will love you."

"I'm happy with who I am," Mariposa declared as she flew to the queen's side with the cure. Queen Marabella awoke, and all of Flutterfield was bright again. The Skeezites screamed in pain and fled, along with the evil Henna. "I'll be back!" she cried.

Queen Marabella was grateful to Mariposa and all her friends for saving Flutterfield. She gave Mariposa, Rayna, Rayla, and Zinzie beautiful fairy headbands as a reward.

Mariposa had never been so happy. She had made special new friends—and discovered just how special she was, too!